Two Small Lives

by Suki

Naked Eye Publishing

First published online at twosmalllives.co.uk 2014
Naked Eye edition published 2015

Book design and typesetting by Naked Eye
Cover illustration by Lois Brothwell

ISBN: 1910981036
ISBN-13: 978-1-910981-03-0

www.nakedeyepublishing.co.uk

Acknowledgements

My heartfelt thanks are owed to all the artists whose work is reproduced in this book. Their names appear beside the artworks, and those who have websites are further listed at the end of this volume. Particular thanks go to Lois Brothwell for providing the cover image and for her moral support and encouragement throughout the 'Suki' endeavour. A special word of gratitude goes to Suki's unfailing muse, Alison Marshall, without whose criticism Suki would be even more of a hopelessly self-obsessed and self-indulgent mess. And last but not least, Suki will forever be indebted to Bel (managed by Michael Kilyon) for lifting her into a new realm and taking the story ever forward.

Two small lives is a work of fiction in which no character represents any living person.

Contents

1. Autumn again..2
2. ...I was a mere flash in Steve's pan....................................4
3. Shipton College: my home-from-home...............................6
4. Sixty-two shopping days to Christmas................................8
5. Saturday: Ian Seed's prose poetry workshop.....................10
6. Sunday: rebound...12
7. Monday..14
8. Tuesday: Hallowe'en...16
9. Piggy-in-the-middle? No thanks.......................................18
10. Disinhibition..20
11. Dragon. Not...22
12. A week later...24
13. A Dom among the Brigg Mill Drawing Group...................26
14. Plumber (1)..28
15. Plumber (2)..30
16. Another prose poem!...32
17. Pensioners' group, Addingley 34
18. SUCCESS, SUCCESS, SUCCESS......................................36
19. Leaving Nathan and Paolo's...38
20. Even though I am happy…..40
21. Friends (1)...42
22. Friends (2)...44
23. 'Flash fiction' competition...46
24. Is this poetry or prose? 48
25. Plumber (3)..50
26. The artist's perspective...52
27. Dougal's studio, snowy December morning.....................54
28. Last Foundation class before Christmas..........................56
29. Christmas Eve..58
30. The dark months..60
31. No period..62
32. Five months?...64
33. The father..66
34. Plan A...68
35. Revised Plan A...70
36. The old ones are the best...72
37. Plan B...74

Struggling writer Suki, still earning her keep working as a model for a motley crew of artists, continues her quest for literary success alongside self-doubt and loneliness in this second part of her autobiographical trilogy.

Liaisons with dissatisfactory males have become part of life since the end of her long-term love-affair with Ilka. Part II opens with Suki alone once again after her latest doomed fling. The ongoing failure to get her novel published is undermining her *raison d'etre*, and with lonely middle-age looming, Suki's soldierly determination wavers. But then, unforeseen events unfold...

Suki's creator Sue Vickerman has received three Arts Council (UK) awards for her poetry, novels and short stories. An international readership has followed Suki's serialised trilogy which may be read at sukithelifemodel.co.uk. Part I, A Small Life, is additionally available in print (Cinnamon Press). Part III, True Life Nude, can be read online at truelifenude.co.uk and its print version will shortly be available (Naked Eye Publishing).

Also by Sue Vickerman

Poetry

Shag
Arrowhead Press, England, 2003
Naked Eye, England, 2015

The social decline of the oystercatcher
Biscuit Publishing, England, 2005

Kunst by 'Suki'
Indigo Dreams Publishing, England, 2012

Thin bones like wishbones by 'Suki' and Sue Vickerman
Indigo Dreams Publishing, England, 2013

Fiction

Special needs, Cinnamon Press, Wales, 2011

A small life, Cinnamon Press, Wales, 2012

Online fiction

asmalllife.co.uk

twosmalllives.co.uk

truelifenude.co.uk

Blog

sukithelifemodel.co.uk

38. Bottom falling out of Plan B...76

39. Sculpted in clay (1)..78

40. Sculpted in clay (2)..80

41. Sculpted in wire..82

42. Thursday..84

43.   3.10 a.m..86

44. March...88

45. Post-Scream...90

46. Dougal's studio, late March...92

47. Abortion pose..94

48. No peace..96

49. Summer..98

50. Tampon string...100

51. Dougal's studio, depleted group, end of June......................................102

52. Young. Not...104

53. London launch 106

54. Post-launch 108

55. Interview on Radio Pepperwharfe (1)...110

56. Interview on Radio Pepperwharfe (2)...112

57. Bluebottles at Brigg Mill...114

58. Rainy Sunday afternoon, Chianti upstairs..116

59. 48th birthday...118

60. The person who knows me best...120

61. Option 1...122

62. Option 2...124

63. Option 3...126

64. Victoria Herz of Brown and Herz Literary Agency..............................128

Contributing artists...130

1. Autumn again

Before you read on, listen to Eva Cassidy singing 'Autumn Leaves'. Put it on continuous play while you pour a whisky. Then open 'Bonjour Tristesse' by Francoise Sagan. Page 1. *A strange melancholy pervades me which I hesitate to give the grave and beautiful name of sadness* (wish I could come up with an opening line for 'Melanie Alone' as fab as that).

Because autumn is about dying. Because my novel has failed to be born. Because life's a bitch. Because…

Kate Stewart

2. …I was a mere flash in Steve's pan

After six weeks, Wife has dumped whoever her fling was and has persuaded Steve to go back to her.

I find a sock of his in my washing machine.

At tonight's session he stays behind me, painting my back. I can't believe he's even showed up. At break-time he rants (oh, but so endearingly…) to whoever will listen, about David Hockney being unable to paint. I focus on (mentally) editing my current poem-in-progress.

So that's that.

Until tonight, this was always my favourite group. It was my very first village hall. I have my own coffee mug here. Bastard.

I wonder if any of the others know about us.

The bloody, bloody greenfly from the Threshington Horticultural Club's stupid tomato plants are driving me crazy. Like motes of dust, almost invisible, creeping on my skin, agonizing. But I *don't move.* Am I the world's greatest life-model?

Douglas Binder

3. Shipton College: my home-from-home

Routine helps with recovery.

A quaint feature of this Art Department is there's never any paper. Like how it must have been behind the Iron Curtain. Bread shortages, paper shortages. Thwarted artists in Eastern Bloc countries.

But this is modern-day Britain that is thwarting creativity; this regime of *Kapitalismus pur*, as my ex Ilka declared before she left.

Tristram, Mr Foundation Course Team Leader, resourcefully has them using newspaper:

'Least the Shipton Herald is still a broadsheet, thank god. Use the fattest brush you can find and two colours of acrylic, a hot one and a cold one. No detail please. You're looking at form, then at light and shade.'

At home I use my empty time to send out a batch of work. Then I book myself onto a poetry workshop. No-one to distract me any more from my vocation.

Who needs a relationship?

Moi, non.

Ich nicht.

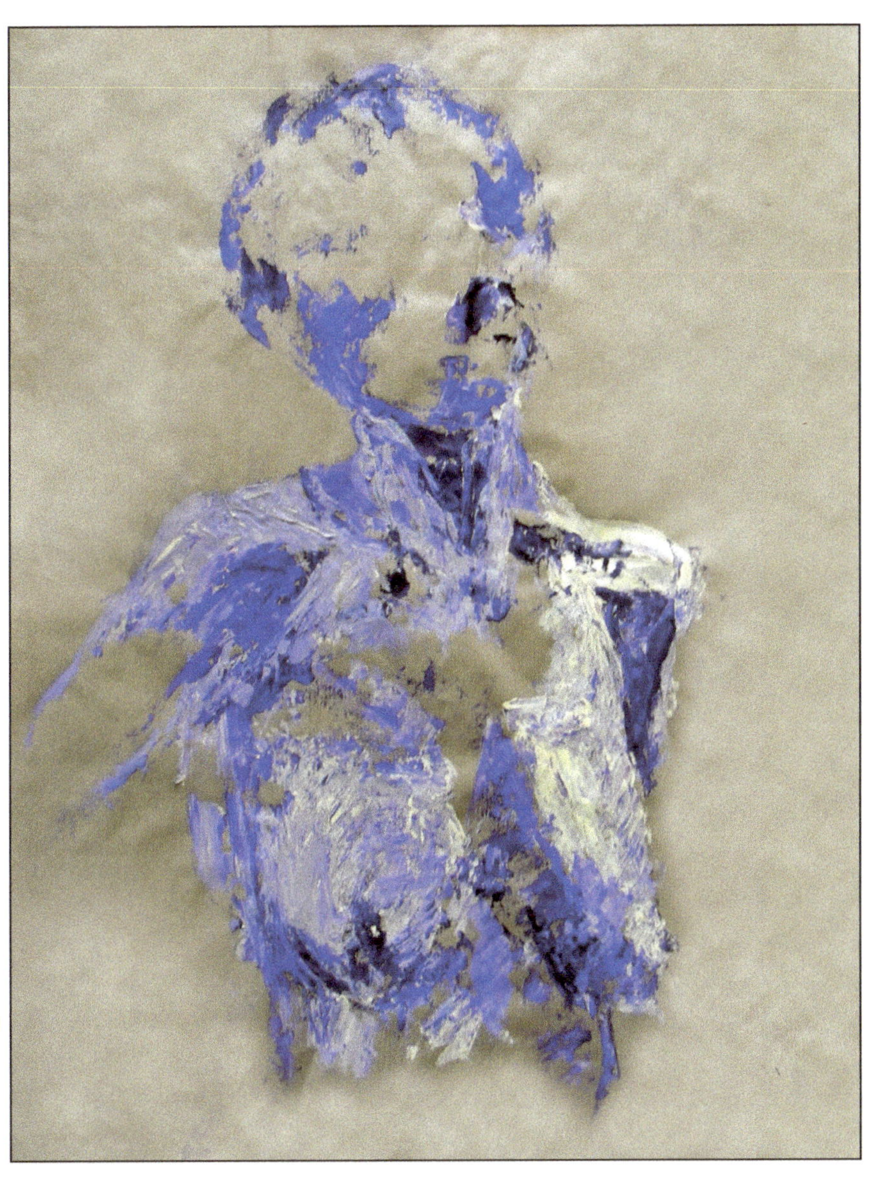

Eliza Dear

4. Sixty-two shopping days to Christmas

Another week survived. A new poem started.

Tristram makes the students draw me at arm's length. Paper on the floor. Long willow sticks dipped into ink in jam-jars.

I look like I'm drawn in blood. *After the brutal axe murder the serial killer leaves his famed signature, a bloody sketch on the bed-sheet's white expanse.*

I'll use that in a story.

Tristram has a wife and kids and a studio in his basement that he never sets foot in. Apparently family life wasn't good for Picasso either.

I am single. I am childless. I am free.

I am lucky.

Julia Jaeger

5. Saturday: Ian Seed's prose poetry workshop

A prose poem is a text which at first glance doesn't look like a poem due to not having the line-breaks of a poem. Printed as prose, it may be a paragraph in length, or have several paragraphs ('stanzas'). It may (or may not) be both right and left justified. It may (or may not) be laid out with more-narrowed-than-usual margins on the page. In surrendering the poet's most valuable tool, the line break, access is gained to a broader palette of syntax and sentence structures. Prose poems are particularly accommodating to poems with a strong narrative line, or a lot of landscape detail – a lot of hard-to-digest data.

I float out of the first session on a high. Ian likes my prose poems.

...looks like prose but features the charged language that is characteristic of poetry, exploiting linguistic resources such as compression, poetic imagery, cadence, fragmentation, non-literal language, rhythms, figures of speech, rhyme, internal rhyme, assonance, consonance. It breaks some of the normal rules of prose discourse in order to achieve a heightened image or emotional effect.

At the bookstall I spend a week's food money on an anthology of British prose poetry and on Simon Armitage's 'Seeing Stars'. Writing is my *raison d'etre*, and books are my food.

A particular structural strategy employed in the prose poem is poetic closure.

Ian says I am good at closure.

I am so much more creative when not distracted by some cheap desperate *affaire du coeur*.

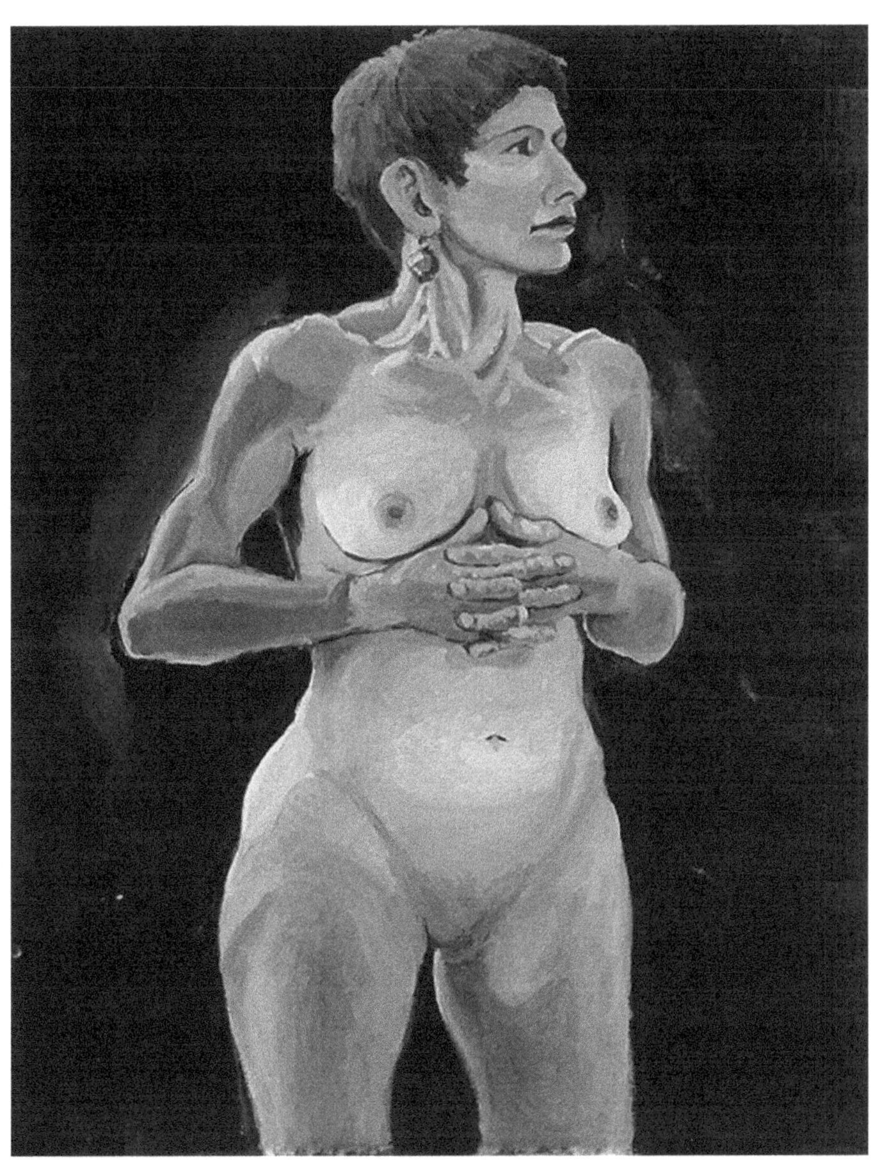

Cathy Everett

6. Sunday: rebound

I am killing time before my twelve noon appointment at the Travelodge
with a man off the internet. (Tiffany - bedsit above mine - showed me the
site). He's going to tie me up.

The Damien Hirst exhibition is a bit small. Disappointing. That's Leeds
for you. Nine exhibits. A token sheep in formaldehyde.

I think it's about life and death and their inconsequentiality. Dead man's
head, dead sheep, body parts in cupboards, skulls, piles of pills with
which to kill oneself. 'Life' being the vibrantly-hued butterflies in
concentric circles: life in cycles. New-agey. Though they're blatantly dead
too. It's all blank and emotionless. But isn't that the *Zeitgeist*? I flip my
poetry notebook closed and drop it back in my bag.

Internet Man has a little daughter who is the light of his day, which keeps
him in his loveless, sexless marriage, which is kind, so I trust him.

To be safe I text Tiff - *if they find me in canal in bin-liner tell em wz Simon
Black of Northallerton*. She texts me - *crazy lady enjoy*.

Tony Noble

7. Monday

Serial fling-ettes are worth it. They stimulate creativity. See this prose poem.

Hotel

What if he has no intention of turning the virtual thing we've had on the internet into reality, so will not be outside Leeds Travelodge at twelve noon when I get there in the businessy-looking outfit he wants me to wear with court shoes; will not emerge from the Travelodge just as I'm retouching my lipstick out of nerves, take me by the elbow and steer me into – no, not straight into the hotel but round the back to where the bins are, to where rubbish has been spread across the alleyway by cats or by an urban fox so that it smells bad in the sun, where he pushes me against the redbrick and speaks in a low menacing voice the kinds of words he writes when we chat online.

What if the national economy crashes today between my departure from home and arrival by train at Leeds, at Leeds Travelodge; something so momentous that public transport stops, or maybe it is a terrorist attack, everything stops, or some sort of magnetic force caused by a comet that makes all the clocks and watches stop, or jolts the world out of its timing, so that twelve noon doesn't even happen and I do not arrive at the Travelodge and will not be taken to the anonymous room he has already booked and paid for, steered by the elbow in an ecstasy (both of us) an ecstasy of anticipation.

What if he forgets the whip. Or doesn't use it. Or doesn't look at all like the name he has given himself so that I cannot bring myself to call him by it. Christ, what if he just downright doesn't want to do it to me after all this, all this talk. What if his wife. His little daughter. What if the civil service department he works for. What if instead I stay on the train past Leeds and end up in a god-awful seaside town in perishing cold looking out at the grey sea, at a lone cockle-picker like a dot on the quicksands, and I feel afraid for that person. Life is so fragile.

Carine Brosse

8. Tuesday: Hallowe'en

Tristram starts the students off with a ten minute warm-up pose. For that length of time I can hold a wacky position. I arch my back, twirl my hands into two spidery shapes, crane my neck, lips parting as my skin pulls taut. Silence falls. The scratch of charcoal begins. I am gazing up past the suspended light-fittings to the leaf-spattered glass of the skylight.

'There's a man.'

'What? Where? O crikey.'

I hear Tristram pluck a board from an easel. He quickly appears beside me, angling the board above his head until it blocks the workman's view.

'Gawd. Can someone go tell them in the office?'

'S'alright, I don't mind. It'll give him an anecdote for the pub.'

Forty-eight hours have passed but my wrists and ankles still have faint pink lines. It looks like where my watch has been. Except it's both wrists. The ankle marks will just be put down to sock elastic.

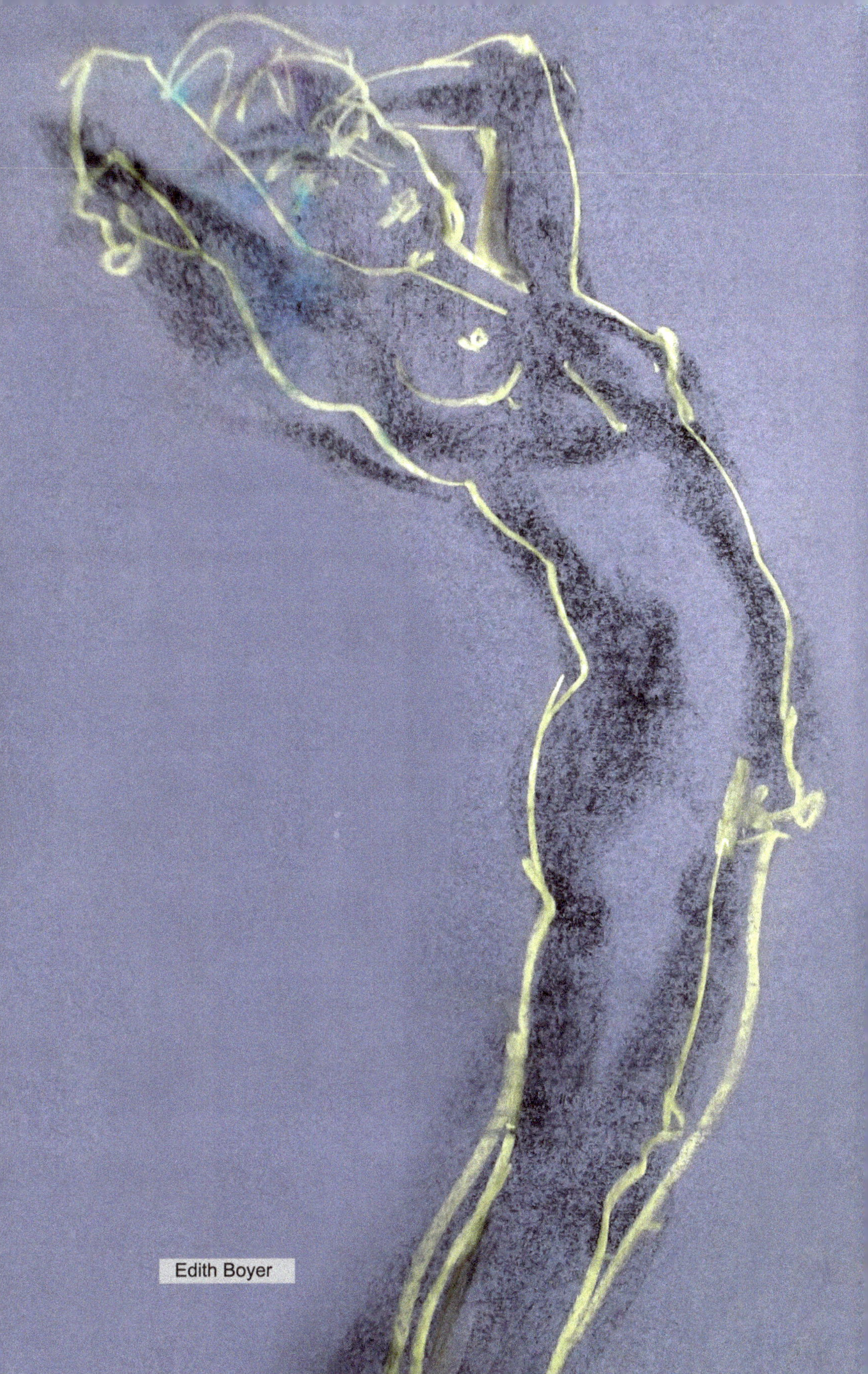
Edith Boyer

9. Piggy-in-the-middle? No thanks.

Ach Du Schreck! As my ex, Ilka, used to say. Tessie with whom I am booked to co-model is off sick; instead it's feminine Marilyn from last year who thought I made a pass at her and was nearly sick.

Petronella sets us up on the mattress. I'll focus anywhere except on Marilyn.

At break-time I see that, just like last year, they are drawing Marilyn as the girl and me as the boy. One punter has even used pink and blue pastels.

The drawings show her to be looking at me. Really intensely. Maybe she's become bi-curious. Ha.

At the end her boyfriend who has come to pick her up comes right in to the life-room, right in to the changing corner before we've finished dressing. It's obviously about a threesome. Obviously his idea.

Which is kind of interesting.

But afterwards I'd be the one leaving, wouldn't I.

Alone.

Susan Forster Ross

10. Disinhibition

Cycling home from Petronella's day-workshop on the busy A650, a sudden gust of wind flaps the front of my skirt right up round my waist. Having been naked in front of fifteen people for five hours, I don't reflexively push it back down. I don't do it for about a minute. I am at first puzzled when a taxi-driver pulls alongside me and coasts, then suddenly -

'O god!'

I revert to normal social behaviour.

Am I going senile?

Colin Morgan

11. Dragon. Not.

I go back to the life-drawing workshop the following Saturday because this is allowed as part-payment for a day's modelling, but I go to make notes for poems, not to draw. I want to observe the dynamic between artists and model from the outside instead of being part of it.

So I get to meet and exchange mobile numbers with another model, a man, who turns out (and I don't know this until I have given him my number) not to be a model but a plumber, who doesn't really have any other contacts so will not be able to help me get more bookings.

But maybe I can get a poem out of him.

At break-time the plumber is reading The Sun. I comment on the Chinese characters tattooed at the base of his back:

'Dragon. I worked in China for a couple of years. I'm a dragon. It's my year.'

'Are you? I am as well!'

It comes round every twelfth year. So he's either twelve or twenty-four years younger than me. Either thirty-five or twenty-three. He looks about halfway between. Maybe he's got the year wrong. Like he's got the characters upside down.

David Thomas

12. A week later

Have ignored all his texts apart from sending one: *tanx 4 inspiration*. Plumber poem completed! Am on a poetry roll. Novel manuscript buried under armchair - no longer dwell on it.

Male model

On a black sheet on a mattress in the quietness
he lies on his back, legs crooked up, dog-like,
looking at the skylight, his navel a slit-eye,
scrotum a bulky pocket, belly a flat white plate
panting a little but now subsiding, penis lazily
flopped as he goes sleepy, jaw slackening.

Nine artists inspect him from drawing boards
propped up on chair-backs or from easels.
Rapt. Muttering. Measuring. Picking out fingers,
his mucky-soled feet; getting his angles, his eyes.
They remake him in charcoal, in soft dark pencil,
the black spideriness of an armpit, of the groin.

A watercolourist paints the faint tee-shirt line
on his extended arm. A painter in oils pulls a fine brush
along a leg, translates him – gentian, aquamarine.
An architect plots out the graph of limbs, torso,
how one thigh divides from the other thigh,
the head's easy tilt, mouth open slightly

as the man dozes, eyes disappeared,
abdomen shallowly rhythmic, the fan heater
sighing to the end of a cycle, clicking off
then clicking on again. A plane flies over.
Someone coughs. The subject's eyes
flicker up to the ceiling again then close

while a pen in the grip of a nail-biter's hand
makes jagged marks around the stark man-shape
on the black sheet, a man asleep
being broken down into the parts of himself,
who is no more nor less than a man;
who is on his back, dog-like.

Tony Noble

13. A Dom among the Brigg Mill Drawing Group

'Are you consciously taking up Gorean slave positions?'

This question is from a regular who in the two-hour session has produced no more than one big triangular scribble: my pubic hair in orange crayon.

I get home from Brighouse and Google Gorean slave positions. The Land of Gor is the cult s-m fantasy fiction series of one John Norman. Inadvertently I have been adopting some of his slave-girl positions. I find some animations on You-tube. Gorean slave girls have manes of long thick hair by which they are pleasurably dragged.

Good poses. I memorise a couple.

Back home I pick up an email booking me for Pepperwharfe. With the plumber.

As always, my need for money overrides all other considerations.

Jane Fielder

14. Plumber (1)

It should not feel like glamour-modelling but it does. Due to Racy Derek (Pepperwharfe group organizer) saying Give us your shoulder blades, Suki. Due to my co-model the plumber having texted me loads ever since he met me, wanting to meet for coffee and "discuss poses". It doesn't take much to flip this activity over into something else.

He stands bluntly, a fence post. I put myself in more of a shape, show muscles, bones, the hollows between them.

Should we be touching?

Keith Lowe

15. Plumber (2)

My back is to the wall. He is seated, looking a bit ungainly. I think there should be some sort of engagement between our two figures, otherwise why not draw us on separate pieces of paper? So I rest a hand on John's shoulder. That's good, says Racy Derek.

I am going to get a prose-poem out of this.

Edith Boyer

16. Another prose poem!

What John does for a living

She is already on the podium, her long tee-shirt discarded, the artists already in front of their papers or behind canvases on easels fingering charcoal or poking at their paints when the new model, John, comes out of the toilet where he went to change as though shy. John who seems nervous and a bit excited, who she found out does not paint in his spare time or even have an interest in art; who is not at all creative (what would the point of her life be if she were not creative) but works for Ellison's all round Harrogate.

Even though her toilet needs mending she makes it quite clear with her body-language that she does not have the remotest interest. Derek is setting them up in the pose he wants; he likes to book a male and a female together sometimes. Some esoteric idea in his mind's eye. He was always like that. For the first half-hour she is standing and John is sitting and she has her hand on his tanned back. The second half-hour she is sitting and he is standing with a hand on her shoulder and she feels his weight shift, he is moving a bit. He is rubbish at it. They can't get the younger-end male models says Derek.

In her head she is working on a poem (one of a series about being childless) because that's what she does, she's a poet, which is why she has always gone for creative types who do not have conventional day-jobs but who live in garrets or on houseboats and don't have tellies or tattoos or sun-tans; pasty-white skinny artists with whom she feels like-minded, who are penniless and utterly incapable of commitment (though intense and passionate, and she insists she would do it all again), who live at an oblique angle to life because life - and this is her hobby-horse - life is not Pizza Hut, is not stag nights in Ibiza or pubic hair cut into shapes or a powerful motor. Three times in the last fortnight this man John has texted her (Derek gave him her number) despite being half her age, wanting to take her for an Indian and discuss poses. Derek, to give him his due, proposed marriage until the miscarriage. He used to sculpt ballerinas when at art college (he said he had a lot of fun with them, something about clamping their nipples with a measuring implement). Her response to John was blunt. John, you're a plumber.

Scuffed wood of the podium. Yellow paint-spot. Their skin making very light contact. On the periphery of her vision, the heap of her black tee-shirt, someone's thermos, the parcel of John's scrotum, Derek a ghost with a twitching brush and oh for god's sake, John's pink adder-head becoming alert.

Though he'll have a high sperm count. And she thinks of the puddle round her toilet. Derek wanted this to happen. You're a bit Pizza Hut yourself, aren't you Derek, a bit Ibiza.

Patricia Oxley

17. Pensioners' group, Addingley

After fantasising about Internet Man (see my prose poem 'Hotel') for a while to get warm, I have a sensation on my inner leg and I know that, if I looked down, I would find a silvery filament has descended from my pubic hair and stickily engaged with the flesh of my thigh. Like a spider letting down its thread, or like Rapunzel letting down a single shiny silvery hair as though saying, come to me, come up to me.

I am as bad as the erectile plumber.

Sue Ibbotson

18. SUCCESS, SUCCESS, SUCCESS

My novel 'Melanie Alone' has won a prize with a small press and the prize is publication.

At long last.

It will come out in July, nine months from now. Like being pregnant.

I take champagne to Paolo and Nathan's back in my old village. On arrival at their sumptuous manor, I find Conservative Jeremy there. Paolo calls him that since I confided in them. CJ is painting Nathan's portrait. So he gets a kiss as well.

CJ won't stay for the champagne because he has a model arriving for a two-hour sitting. I say, come back to us after. He says he'll see how he feels. He slopes off.

'Do you think he'll come back?'

'He's probably shagging his model, Suki.'

'I honestly don't think he shags every model.'

'He was a bastard to you. Here's your champagne, well done darling.'

'We should save some for him just in case.'

'Stop it!'

Yvonne Hurley

19. Leaving Nathan and Paolo's

Cycling to the station for the last train I do a detour round the village to pass Conservative Jeremy's cottage. The light is on in his studio. I had wine after the champagne. I am so happy I won't be bothered if the bastard doesn't let me in. It's worth at least ringing the doorbell, in case he does.

He does.

Jill Moynan

20. Even though I am happy…

The Playhouse Life-drawing Club takes place in the grungy theatre bar with a barman who likes to watch. The Playhouse is on the verge of bankruptcy. The tables haven't been wiped since the cleaners stopped being paid. The podium is theatrically spot-lit. Marlene Dietrich is singing. Helga, who is my fan (*fantastic definition! Can't get enough of you!*), gives me costumes to put on from the theatre's wardrobe and they make me pose on a rickety sideboard. In the break someone gets me a dry white wine.

Change of music. I am back on the sideboard with wine in my veins when Dido's song 'Thank you' starts up. I know it from the lesbo movie 'If These Walls Could Talk', the scene where Sharon Stone and Ellen Degeneres have sex after Sharon has been inseminated at the gay-friendly fertility clinic, hoping for third time lucky.

I watched it with my ex Ilka about a million times when I was backwards and forwards to the Aberdeen clinic. I had twelve goes, not three.

In the next scene they are in the bathroom testing Sharon's pee. There's this agonizing moment of watching for the little line to appear - will it, won't it - then they go ecstatic and dance about.

My eyes swim. I try blinking. I try not blinking. One tear pops out. It's just an *auld lang syne* tear.

Ilka claimed that DVD, thank god.

Glenn Hall

41

21. Friends (1)

After a minute the other swimmy eye overflows too. They must be visible under this spotlight. But I wouldn't react either, if I were the artists. It would bring about the end of the pose.

While I'm getting dressed, Helga (who as a fan is included on my list of 'friends') puts her arm round my shoulder.

'You alright? Thought you were in celebratory mood?'

'I'm fine! Jonathan's blinking turps was right up my nose.'

Janey Walklin

22. Friends (2)

Tiffany upstairs needs me at least in practical ways. She has been for her penis removing at last and a vagina putting in. I've been feeding Oedipuss while she was in hospital.

She shows me her new genitalia, then we look at Guardian Soulmates online. Some are quite nice. Since we are both open to either a woman or a man (how flexible is that), Tiff suggests going halves on a subscription.

'But I'd only tick 'fling' for myself, Tiff. You want the whole big *affaire d'amour.*'

'I don't believe you just want a fling. The way you go on about Conservative Jeremy.'

'CJ? Pah! He was just a shag.'

'I don't know how you could have gone to bed with a Conservative.'

' The 'C' isn't his politics. He only does missionary position.'

'I'd love that.'

'Anyway I'm deffo not ready for another seventeen-year joined-at-the-hip thing like with Ilka.'

'Oh, I want joined-at-the-hip. I want forever. I want the love of a good woman. Or a knight on a white horse.'

Chris Murray

23. 'Flash fiction' competition

I will have a go at this. Big prize money. Might be lower odds than the poetry competitions. Not that there's much difference, anyway, between a piece of short fiction and a prose poem (– is there?).

They've set a limit of five hundred words. Tell a whole story within that constraint.

I want to achieve what Tracey Emin has achieved in her latest exhibition of herself in all her nakedness.

Douglas and his ageing curmudgeonly fellow-artists love to slag her off as being unable to draw. She herself proclaims that she can't draw, but I think these blunt, raw gouache paint-drawings – and the sculptures – are primitively, sophisticatedly, elegantly, vulgarly, confidently amazing.

Her true purpose is to communicate passion, says her Guardian reviewer (albeit a tad sycophantically). *Her works share epiphanies of love and loneliness…*

That's me! What *I* write about! *Me! My* life…

The point is, it's everybody's life, isn't it.

Tell me.
Tell me it's not your life.

For the competition I will retell my story – the perennial story – of love, of loneliness. Make them laugh and cry. Reach a dramatic crescendo. Then a grand finale.

Above all, win some dosh.

Joanne Hogg

24. Is this poetry or prose?

More to the point, will it win me some money? I want to buy myself the odd Christmas present. And Tiff. And Bel, as a thank-you for all those lovely little docu-films she's been making of art groups drawing me.

Ecological disaster

I find it after six months have passed, when I decide to take down the last of her pencil drawings, underneath which is another one, taped up on the wall in her neat way. Oh my god. There, superimposed on one of the dozens of sketches she drew of the outside of me is a drawing of the inside of me. After everything that failed to happen, after everything that didn't get said.

She has invented - I say invented because she hasn't a clue what my inside is like - an unscientific sort of network of veins in pink, blue and lime green. Not my colours at all but then she doesn't know what's really in there; she never studied me well enough to know what my colours or tastes are and she never asked. So those colours are wrong.

The network of veins she has drawn inside me is as flimsy and delicate as a spider's web whereas CJ's depiction of the inside of me is more towards the boldness of the London Underground map because CJ thinks that's how I function, all Broadway Boogie Woogie, but again, all those bright bold colours are wrong. And the edges ought to blur out, but CJ is far too anal retentive to let that happen.

Perhaps I should be flattered that she perceived this sensitive-looking lacy fragility inside me. I evidently came across to her as complicated. If John on the other hand were to draw my insides he would draw a concrete network of motorways like Spaghetti Junction along which steam-rollers trundle, along which bulldozers bulldoze. A messy grey scribble with no flair or subtlety, the lack of which is no reflection on me but rather speaks volumes about John, who is not an artist but a plumber who can only visualise basic pipe systems. He would build me in Meccano alright but that's as far as it could ever go.

Black canals is me. That stagnant network that joins up post-industrial cities. I am dark arteries. The black worms of my veins spewing out indelible ink when cut open. Ironically it is John who has a bit of insight into the sluggish passage of liquid along channels, who has the practical skills to steer along these waterways. The time I got cut by one of the above (I'll leave you to puzzle it out - not John, obviously) was more devastating than today's oil-spill which has already obliterated the sea-life of a whole ocean and the bird-life of half a continent, the full ramifications of which we cannot yet even guess at.

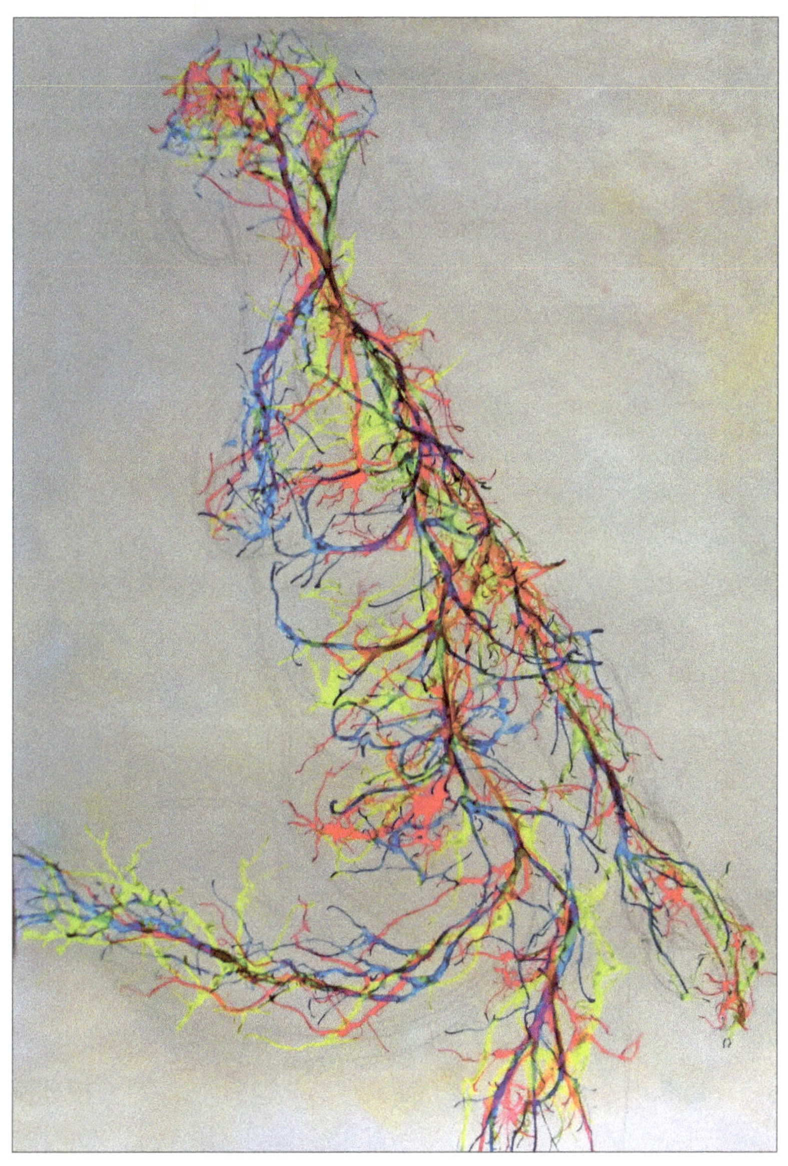

Sheila Overton

25. Plumber (3)

'So what you doing for Christmas Suki?'

'I'll be working hard on my next poetry collection. Great opportunity to hunker down and get some work done. No disruption. Bliss.'

'A quiet one, then.'

'Yes.'

'Very nice. I like a bit of a party, me. Anyway if you want some more fun you've got my number.'

I cold-shoulder him, obviously. Though when I was lying back to back with him, I did enjoy the warmth.

It is December 6th. Before bed I check my inbox for a St Nikolaus Tag greeting from Ilka.

There is one solitary message. The subject box says *Early Christmas gift*. I open the email.

Just completed that other film short. Watch it here. Happy Advent! Bel x

The film is of a one-to-one booking I had with an artist called Patricia Oxley. The music – Schubert's *Voyage Magnifique* - is interspersed with Pat talking about her use of projections and light. Some of Bel's shots could be categorized as 'art nude' photography.

Bel is branching out. I really like what she does. I'd like to get to know her better. A new friend!

Great movie – thank you! Wd u like meet up – pre-Xmas drink?

An out-of-office message comes back:

I am working in Shanghai and unable to respond to emails.
Kind regards.
www.bel-photography.co.uk

I go to her website and, from there, to a new link: 'Shanghai blog'. But it gives away nothing.

Bel is a mystery.

John Bolland

26. The artist's perspective

I tried to stand in Conservative Jeremy's shoes to write this poem but it
was too hard to describe my own body, so I became a female artist and
described CJ's body.

What the artist habitually does with her one-night stands

Afterwards, she draws them,
pen moving over the dome of this one's
abdomen then travelling up it,
blocking in his man-breasts,
a broad shoulder, biceps,
the angle between arm and torso

wondering whether to see him again.
Now sweeps down, leaves a light trail of ink –
his back, his hip; sketches the dark mess of
hair and sac and member, reaches once more
to the big square shoulder, that thick neck,
the bulldog look of this man's cropped head,

how his fingers are small and splay a little,
her skin remembering; her hands remembering
his boneless hips. She picks out the delicate
textured points of his nipples, the ring in his ear,
his indeterminate hairline, wondering why his lips
are uncertain; why, behind his eyes, that shadow.

Edith Boyer

27. Dougal's studio, snowy December morning

'Humph. How fleshy is she?'

'I can't remember. She'd better not be like that one last year.'

'The one that was like a ball on two sticks. I couldn't draw her! I gave up!'

I am in pose. It seems Dougal and his pals (Bradfordian bohemians, pushing seventy) have even booked a model for between Christmas and New Year. That's how fanatical they are. Good for her if she's got fat on her in this freezing place.

But they only like stick-women. They are all scrawny sticks themselves. Especially Rowan the Buddhist who lives on a barge and eats seaweed and apparently not much else, who keeps (discreetly) inviting me to his boat. But I can't be doing with spirituality. And seventy's like, nearly a hundred.

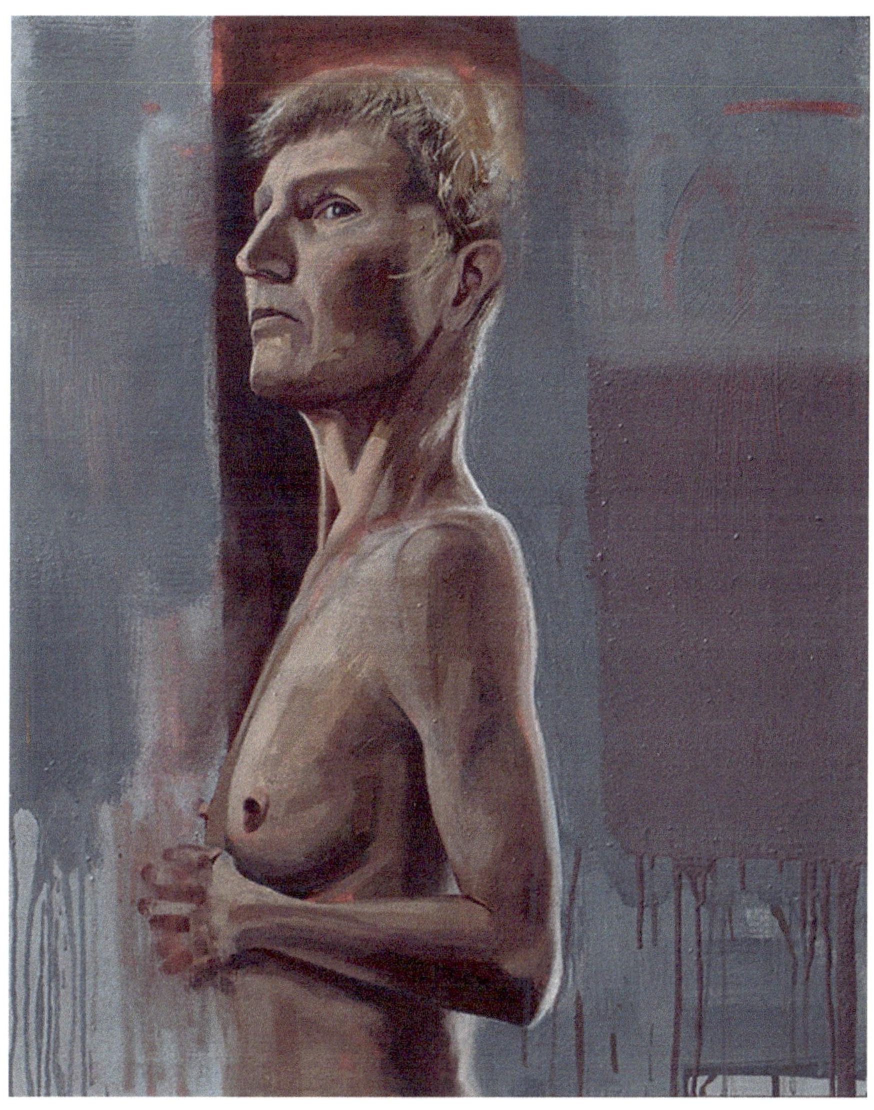

Tom Wood

28. Last Foundation class before Christmas

'Very Euan Uglow.'

When Tristram says these things I hurry home and google the artist. I find an Adrian Searle article from The Guardian: 'Touch is suppressed and pleasure is deferred,' says Ade.

The student whose drawing was very Uglow has just had a 'neck dive' done. A diamante stud implanted into her skin at her neck's nape. It looked sore. *Not* very Uglow. I cannot imagine her even for one nano-second suppressing touch or deferring pleasure.

'Mechanical notations' and 'surveyor's plot-lines', says Ade of Uglow.

Last night a retired architect drew me with lots of little crosses and measurements all over the place. I looked like the plan of a house. Is that Uglow-esque?

Uglow would apparently insist he looked at a life model no differently from any other kind of object, but Adrian says his paintings definitely show a distinct interest in nipples, bums and pubic hair. And 'he had a real thing for putting a naked model in an awkward pose.' What's wrong with that? Flipping burgers on minimum wage hurts too. We models are paid relatively well. We *should* suffer.

Horribly bleak… its rules, its measurements, its endless difficulty, its unsmiling pleasures.

That sounds like Conservative Jeremy.

From whom I have not heard.

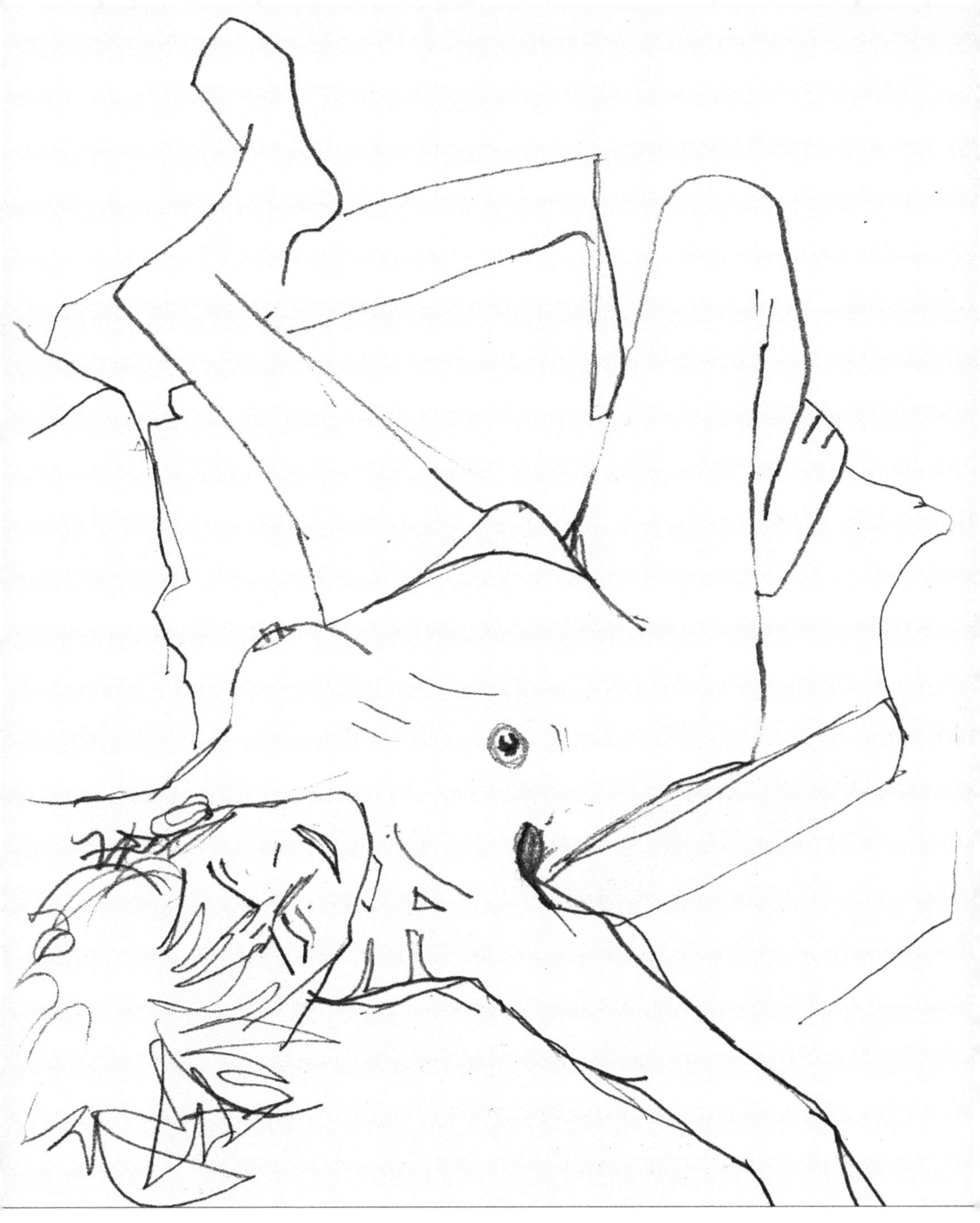

Helen Peyton

29. Christmas Eve

The rare chance to write uninterrupted. No modelling bookings. Just me in my flat. Brilliant.

Think I'll just pop out though and stretch my legs.

Canal Christmas – a prose poem

At the carol service during While Shepherds Watched - still undecided about how best to get through the next forty-eight hours - I am re-living being Gabriel: the frock made of a sheet that I tripped on while climbing up the back of the crib-scene to get above the baby and open out my sheet-wings. How magical it all once was.

The vicar talks about protest, loneliness, corporate greed, his face up-lit by a candle. I don't know what righteousness means. Saviour I understand as a basic human need. When he reads about those who live in a land of deep darkness, I know that place. When he ends with the promised advent of the Prince of Peace, I want that man

but instead I meet up with you at the anti-capitalist encampment in Centenary Square. Bright snow has cleaned everything; sky glittery, incredible, behind Sheryl on her makeshift platform addressing passers-by about a better world. *We are you*, she cries out to the dark city, but only the two of us plus a homeless Polish builder smoking in front of the tents hear her, and it is anyway far too cold

so here I am, after all, on your houseboat parked in a canal basin, hanging lights round this cactus, putting out a stocking for a man who doesn't even do Christmas, who is off alcohol but I nonetheless open champagne

and in the morning you are embarrassed that I have filled you such a big sock that spills everywhere, gift-wrapped packages interspersed with little chocolate Santas although you're also off sugar. I say - just a few bits, it's nothing, thinking, no sock big enough for everything I want to give you out of guilt at feeling so sad; you saying - I really love you; me saying - oh Rowan, don't, and as we're having sex (all the little gifts getting re-parcelled in duvet), as someone embarrassingly calls out Merry Christmas from the towpath, my eyes are closed; I may never come to this houseboat again

but, obliviously happy, you take me to the Festival of Political Song at the anarchist squat where a reunited nineteen-eighties women's chorus is singing new lyrics about menopause symptoms as well as the old ones about men's inadequacies, till a Marxist rocker I vaguely know takes over, his theme exploitation: call-centre workers, cockle-pickers. He does a big strum for the end of the socialist dream but grins as though there is no greater thing on Christmas night than to play a guitar on this podium on the second floor of a derelict woollen mill; these women who are newly grandmothers, this man who sells car parts; he, the boy in the playground who would pinch my arm or ignore me altogether when I tried to play at fainting, when all I wanted was to be saved.

Tom Wood

30. The dark months

Eat, jog it off. Eat, jog it off.

I feel bloated. Maybe because I have eaten seven apples. I often eat seven apples, though, without getting this melon belly.

Tonight's drawings make me look obese. I must start jogging in the evening as well as the morning. But February is still so dark so early.

The best models are skin and bone, aren't they?

John Macfarlan

31. No period

I get the test done at the doctor's to save money on buying the kit. I think it's most likely the menopause but it turns out I am pregnant.

'So how do you feel about this?'

The locum seems interested in me. I suppose because the waiting room is otherwise full of drug-users and obese females with toddlers, same old same old.

'Well. The statistical likelihood of my carrying it to full term at the age of forty-seven - that's if I decide to, if the amniocentesis and everything shows there's nothing wrong with it – it's only thirty per cent or something, isn't it?'

'You're obviously quite genned up already.'

'Internet last night. Not really. A bit.'

'Well at five months gone you've missed your first scan. I'll get you an appointment.'

Janey Walklin

32. Five months?

So, counting back from February, conception was at the end of the summer. Or October.

I've got up this morning looking pregnant. What if people notice?

Sarah Hodgson

33. The father

It could be Conservative Jeremy or it could be Internet Man. Or - tacky, I know - the plumber. Maybe it could even be Steve? I count back and count back. Count, re-count.

Bel texts - evidently back from Shanghai (since when?), wanting to make another of her fly-on-the wall movies of me.

GOD NO. Not when I look like this.

Sandra Cowper

34. Plan A

Go it alone. Not one small saddo life any more but two happy little lives.

Tiffany can be my birth-partner. Ha! That'll show her what being a woman is.

And I've decided to confide in Bel, because we're the same. I mean, about the same age. Unmarried. Alone. Childless (thus far). Well, I *think* she's all those things.

But I get no response to my text. Is she annoyed I didn't reply to her request to make another movie? Has she buggered off back to Shanghai? I visit her UK blog and her Shanghai blog but I can't work out where she currently is. Maybe she's dead.

Is it more difficult to establish new friendships when one is older?

Or is it just me who is rubbish at it?

Lois Brothwell

35. Revised Plan A

By the early hours of the morning I have decided to write a letter to the person who, according to my calculations, is the father. I post it first thing, first class, then go up to Tiffany with my news.

'No more wee drams then, lovey! No more pill-popping! How do you feel? Apart from terrified, obviously?'

'Truly happy. If this isn't a *raison d'etre* I don't know what is.'

Philip Hadwin

36. The old ones are the best

'I didn't recognize you with your clothes on.'

'Ha ha! Could I draw out thirty pounds please.'

I get this one-liner at least once a week. The building society clerk today; a postman on his rounds tomorrow; a woman walking her dog. I never recognize any of them.

I take my little fistful of life savings back to the Oxfam shop which has got this most amazing antique lace christening gown at a rip-off price but I want it so much. I'll probably be able to get a pram for less.

It won't exactly be a christening, what with me not being religious. But something; some naming thing. A massive celebration, anyway.

In Franco's I start a name list on a paper napkin.

And that's where I pick up his text.

'Imposs. Soz.'

John Allcock

37. Plan B

Sunday. Bright and early I write a note to Rowan and do a gentle half-hour jog through the snow to his towpath mailbox. He will return from his Buddhist retreat tonight.

There are spent fireworks from New Year along the canal. The world is still asleep. When I get back, my bedsit looks forlorn, and is freezing. But hopefully I won't, after all, need to fill in these forms and get onto the housing list.

I'd like to go straight back out. Meet a pal. Drink coffee. Commiserate about our crap Christmases. Have a laugh. I'm sick of Tiffany and talking about make-up.

I can't text Bel again. Not when she snubbed my last one.

I put on my dressing-gown and gloves and return to bed.

David Whiting

38. Bottom falling out of Plan B

Thanks for sharing about your pregnancy. I enjoyed Christmas Day (for once!), enjoying drawing you and making love to you with your round fecund belly, and am surprised now that it never occurred to me that there were three beings, not two, on my boat. This has been a big shock for me. Bang go all my fantasies! I have been meditating this evening, during which time your child's spirit visited me asking me to be her father... Perhaps you were able to sense this... But I gently returned her to your care.

I would like us to go on being acquainted, although your focus in life is obviously not, after all, going to be me!! I have had my children. I can't go there again at the age of 69!!! Enjoy your wonderful new adventure, and I promise that I will be here for you as a loving friend. Rowan x

Neil Massey

39. Sculpted in clay (1)

I am reclining on a blanket on one of those shaky wallpapering tables in Pepperwharfe Community Centre. A dozen chatty punters are sketching me.

'Cheer up Suki, it might never happen!'

I do not even know until first break that a woman is kneeling silently at my feet, sculpting them. It feels biblical.

This morning I had the ultrasound. The sonographer called another sonographer, then the midwife, then the obstetrician. They pointed out markers. A strawberry-shaped head. An echogenic bowel. An abnormal heart.

So I let them take a sample of my womb's fluid. The results will be there in two days, and then I have to decide.

Keith Hanselman

40. Sculpted in clay (2)

They are far more beautiful than my real feet.

In the middle of the night I go on my netbook. The markers mean Edwards Syndrome. They are born dead or they just live for a few hours.

Jane Hurford

41. Sculpted in wire

Tristram is talking about artist Alec Calder who worked from a life model to create the most amazing images out of wire. He makes the students have a go.

I crook one leg and one arm to give their pliers some work, and place my other hand on my belly in which this morning's medication is swilling around, preparing the body to give birth. In two days they will be able to induce labour.

For once I'm in a pose where I can yawn, move my eyes. Then someone puts on that Eva Cassidy song I play when I'm drinking and wallowing. Autumn Leaves. I want them to switch it off, but I don't say. A text tinkles into my mobile…

At break I see that the text is from Bel. *Apols, been busy, cn we meet?*

Nope.

Soz, just off on hol! Let u know when home.

At the end of the class I tell Tristram I have a funeral so can't do this Thursday.

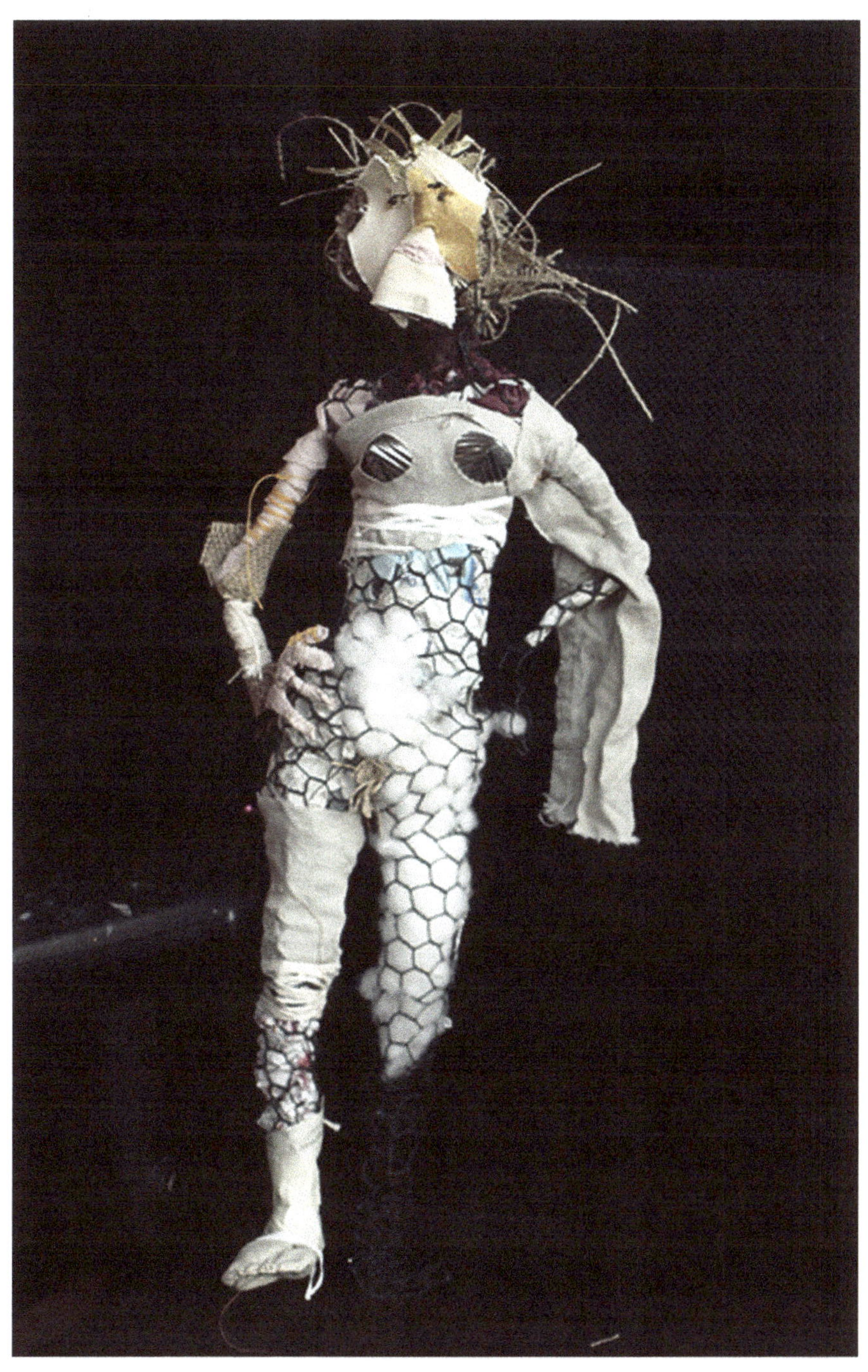

Emma Whiting

42. Thursday

Once it starts, I lose any sense of time.

The sky goes dark.

Towards the end I ask for the morphine.

Phil Moody

43.   3.10 a.m.

'What his name would have been? Please, just take it away.'

David Mace

44. March

I am clearing out my stuff, I think I might need to move away and start again so I am clearing out my stuff, and there's a box of my theology books from uni. I leaf through a Saul Tulloch that used to be important.

You do not know where you have come from, or where you are going. The state of your whole life is estrangement from others and yourself. Estrangement from the origin and aim of your life. Estrangement from the depth and the greatness, while drawing on - living on - the very power-source from which you are estranged.

...But you cannot escape the bindings. You are inextricably bound to your Self and to all other life. Separated and yet bound; estranged and yet belonging; not believing in life, in the life-force, yet being alive. It's a sickness; one that you feel only death will end.

Yes, so I'm toying with that option, okay? You head-fucker.

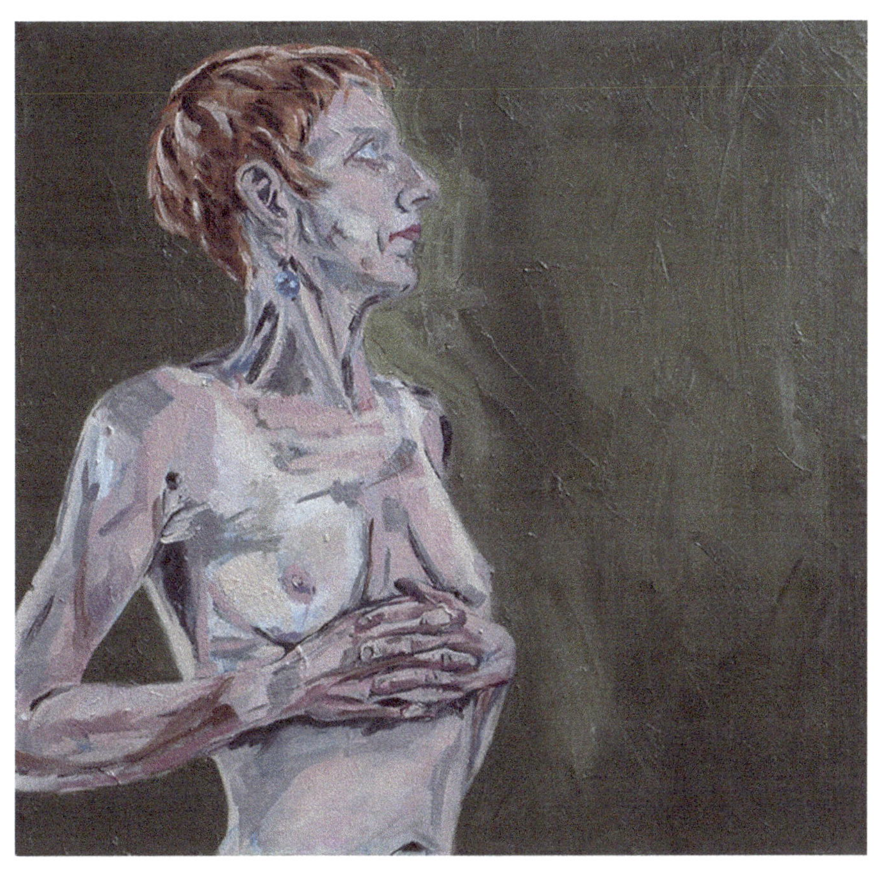

Fiona Halliday

45. Post-Scream

The painting-from-life workshop is a six-hour marathon. The end products are awesome. Phyllis's painting looks like Edvard Munch's model, or what she would have looked like after all that screaming. I snap it on my mobile and send it as a picture-message to my publisher as a possible cover design for 'Melanie Alone'.

My publisher's reply states in the strongest terms that it is a complete no-no.

Brenda Head

46. Dougal's studio, late March

Rowan hugs me.

'Suki. I'm really really sorry. The group thinks you've just had a nasty flu. I've been thinking about you a lot. Come to my boat again. Please.'

As I'm unfolding my bicycle at the end, he puts a note in my hand. At home I read his quite good poem.

Life-model

and I wonder, as I paint her singleness -
so poignantly alone, up there on the podium
in the freezing studio where the rest of us
have kept our coats on, her skin pimpled, bluish,
seeing a quiver ripple up her I wonder whether
taking off her clothes, boots and ear-rings
and ridding her mouth of lipstick (she does this;
wipes it off on her forearm leaving her face stark naked)
whether letting her body be so coldly looked at,
strip lighting so harsh, so unforgiving, whether
letting herself be treated so badly - all our eyes
poking into her in this bare, chilly art-room -
is an act of madness, or a mid-life crisis
or her crying out like a masochist *Hurt me.*

Martin Hannavy

47. Abortion pose

I am clambering about on the arm-chair, testing out poses.

'Very Paula Rego.'

The comment makes me stop. 'Okay, would you like me to go with this one?'

It is fine for twenty minutes. Then it becomes agonising. They want it for four hours. After the first break-time I prop my watch against the fan heater. I watch the minutes. I aim for twenty minute stints before having to spoil their concentration by moving my left leg.

By the afternoon I am watching the seconds, struggling to last five minutes before apologetically shaking my bloodless leg again and shifting my twisted shoulder. I am letting them down. My reputation as a good model is in tatters.

As it happens, this morning at three I was browsing Paula Rego on my netbook.

Keith Lowe

48. No peace

New booking. Workers' Educational Association life-class at the Bickerthwaite United Reformed. The group gets off to a slow start even though I was ready for kick-off dead on the hour. It is chatty, noisy. They are used to having an ongoing repartee with the model. Their accuracy must be shit if they don't mind a model whose face is moving. I bet they're rubbish at hands and feet.

Stop talking to me, people. I want to be inside my head. Please. Leave me alone.

Straight after modelling I go for my counselling session. Conveniently, the Mental Health Services Area Office is behind this very church. It's a Portacabin. Beside the entrance I crouch to lock my bicycle. The rickety door slams open, clunks closed. A previous client hurries away. When I straighten up, I see that it was Bel.

At home I put on Bach's suite for solo cello in G major. I love how a solitary gifted person's use of a tool makes this beautiful sound.

I am an artists' tool. It's good, being a tool. It's a *raison d'etre.*

I play the prelude over and over and over and over. All through the night.

Russell Lumb

49. Summer

Back to normal.

I wake up with a sticky feeling. My belly is like a melon, tight as a drum, a fruit with juice sloshing about in it.

I scrub the blood out of my futon and try drying it with my hairdryer. Thanks to the June warm spell my bedsit window has dehydrated enough to un-jam. I open it to help with the drying then set off on my bicycle for the Foundation class.

A period. An especially bloody one, and yet purposeless, like the pointless and annoying existence of wasps. God having a laugh.

Is bleeding while modelling 'performance art'?

Tony Bulley

50. Tampon string

When I take off my knickers in the art room the long blue coil of it tickles my thigh. Blast. Forgot to snip it short. I never just push the string inside myself because it could easily drop down again. Am I shy? No. I just feel it's Too Much Information.

There is an image by Susan Sontag's partner, photographer Annie Leibovitz, of a naked dancer bending to lace her ballet shoe, thus revealing her 'secret' - her tampon string. It is said to indicate her delicacy and vulnerability.

I finish pulling on my black tee-shirt dress and run to the Ladies with another tampon hidden in my fist. I yank out the current one, pull the plastic casing off the new one, bite through the string near the top and shove it in.

I'll have to rummage to get it out.

Julia Jaeger

51. Dougal's studio, depleted group, end of June

It is good to be a stick-woman again. My belly completely flat. Concave, in fact. Like the skinny cover image for 'Melanie Alone' that the publisher finally chose.

'Was a nice surprise to see you last week Suki. Well you know what I mean. Not a nice occasion, but nice that such a lot of folk showed up for Rowan.'

I don't ever answer when I'm in pose. Just do a faint smile.

'Aye, that was a good wake on the towpath. Fancy managing to fit a marquee onto a towpath.'

Why do artists top themselves?

On the way home I cry a bit, but when I arrive I find on the doormat a small package. My first copy of my novel!!!

'TIFF! You up there?'

Claire Gains

52. Young. Not.

Warm June has nose-dived into better-take-a-jacket July. In Addingley Memorial Hall the pensioners' group keep their fleeces on. When I get into pose I am still steaming from cycling. They are impressed with my fitness. They make remarks about my being youthful.

I do not cool off. My cycling sweat dries but I go on producing heat. The small of my back prickles with new perspiration. I wonder at what age hot flushes start.

In the break I produce my novel and wave it about. They say things like, Ey up – you'll be t' next JK Rowling – and hand me my cup of tea.

Chris Murray

53. London launch

'Thank you, everybody, for coming to the launch of my debut novel 'Melanie Alone'. This is a small step for the world but a huge one for Suki. It's my baby.'

Sarah Hodgson

54. Post-launch

London is great.

After the launch nothing happens. I switch my mobile back on. There's a text from my old pal from uni who hasn't turned up.

V v sorry, hd 2 don dog collar n go hold hand of dying patient. Nex time yr down DEFFO meet xxx

The publisher has rushed off to get the last train back to Wales.

So I go to Friday night 'Late At The Tate' and turn round with my glass of wine and peanuts to find myself dwarfed below the thunderous hulk of Gordale Scar. Like actually being there, but darker. I've never stood in front of the real Gordale Scar in the dark. I feel proud but also defensive: my landscape, my heritage, my spiritual home being ignored by these tinselly London yuppies and clueless foreigners; this live jazz band making lazy sexy light of it. I AM A NORTHERNER you bunch of elitist bastards who won't let me into your world.

Then I am in Paolo and Nathan's designer friend Gary's Barbican shag-pad in my sleeping bag and he is through the wall shagging this little oriental guy and I have my vibrator in my sleeping bag with me and the prospect of a really good designer-shag-pad espresso for breakfast before I get the coach home. It's been great. Well, quite good.

Nick Holmes

55. Interview on Radio Pepperwharfe (1)

When not DJ-ing, Tamara is a personal trainer and life-coach-to-the-wealthy. In her black trouser suit her body looks like whiplash. She rejects Bach's cello solo in G major from my pre-prepared request list. I enthuse about its special characteristic. She is keenly interested. But her listeners, she says, are elderly females who don't have orgasms. She relaxes me with chat. Her leg shifts under the desk, touching mine. Then we go live.

'Themes? Well, my main ones are loneliness, obviously, plus what it's like to fail to find one's *raison d'etre*. And of course the search for love, because isn't that what all stories are about in the end?'

Tamara has okayed the Eva Cassidy. She puts on Autumn Leaves, and pulls off her earphones.

'What I'd like to go onto after this track Suki is questions about how far 'Melanie Alone' is really about 'Suki Alone'; like, the loneliness theme, and how this relates to being a single woman in today's world, which of course both you and Melanie are. Will that be okay?'

'I often get asked to clarify that. I'm totally happy to talk about that. It's inevitable that one draws on one's own experience.'

'Don't tell me now! Wait for the light to come on again...'

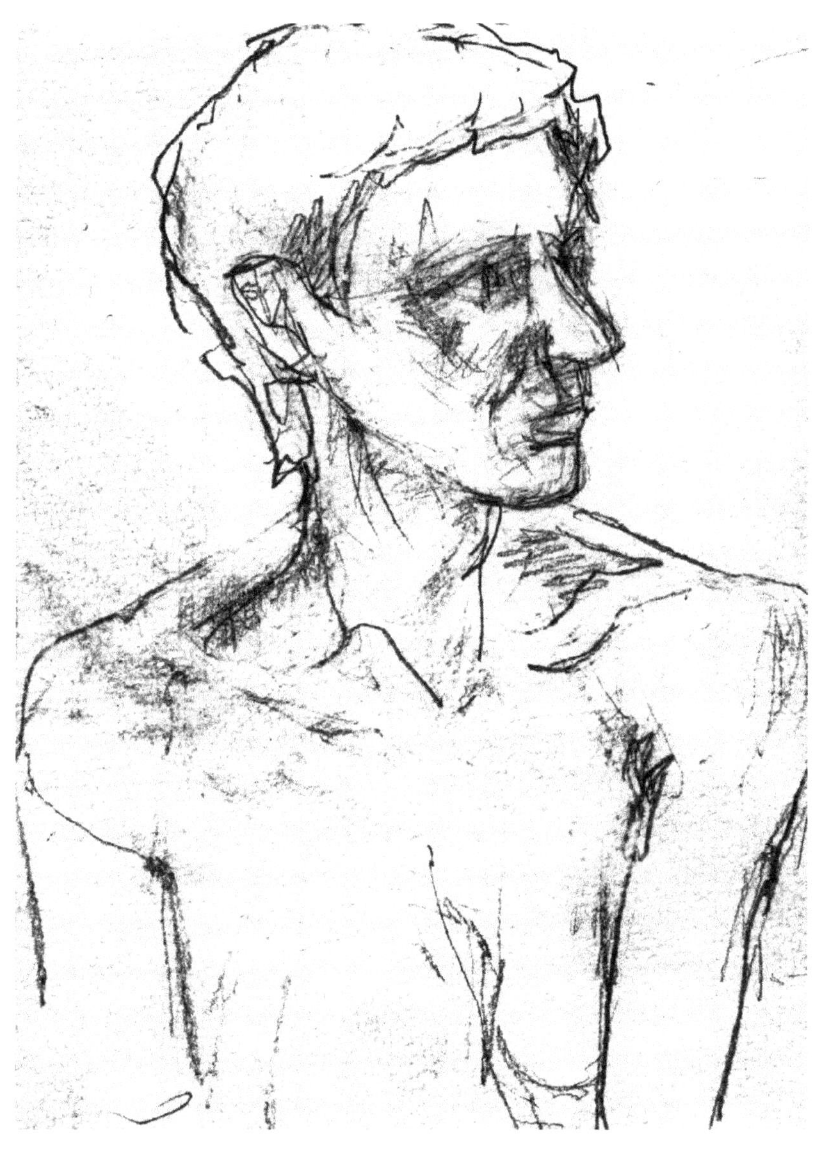

Jo Thompson

56. Interview on Radio Pepperwharfe (2)

'So my question to you, Suki, is: have you ever been taunted yourself, as Melanie is constantly viciously taunted by her mother, for being self-obsessed, selfish and unnatural in choosing not to have children? Has this been an issue for you?'

Sophie Pope

57. Bluebottles at Brigg Mill

They are not as bad as the greenfly at Threshington but they are pretty bad. At least the punters can see them and will sometimes come and waft them off me.

One lands in my pubic hair and potters about among the curls. I do not move a muscle.

Home again I check emails.

I am sorry for that debacle. Your reaction was most unexpected and left me ashamed.

To be honest I was projecting. I have my own issues re that subject, which you don't want to know about. I've had a telling-off from the radio co-op's committee due to listeners' complaints. Everyone on your side. Mea culpa.

Moving on: you are self-evidently a person who does not feed yourself adequately. This needs taking in hand. I will take you out to dinner on Tuesday. Email me back with your address and I'll pick you up. Tamara

Paul Keen

58. Rainy Sunday afternoon, Chianti upstairs

'You're letting that bitch take you out? After that nasty interview fiasco?'

'She's rich. She's gorgeous. And she's the looking-after type; I want to be looked after. And I haven't had sex with a woman for nearly three years.'

Tiffany's situation is far worse than mine. Being under the roof, she gets the leaks. They are about to chuck her off Disability Living Allowance. Oedipuss has cat breast cancer. The view from her bedsit is the Asda car-park. Her new genitalia remain untested.

'Tiff - is there anything you miss about being Timothy?

'My family.'

Joan Dearnley

59. 48th birthday

I have the life of a circus clown, hopping on and off a stupid folding bicycle and taking my clothes off all over the place. I cut a ridiculous figure. A woman my age. My peers all getting excited about being grandmas.

To date, 'Melanie Alone' has had no reviews.

What am I doing? Why? Gimme the whisky. Gimme the pills.

Jeremy. Sometimes I wish there were a place to visit you. A grave.

Roger Hitchen

60. The person who knows me best

'I thought you'd sound slurry by now. I know what your birthday does to you.'

'Ilka! Thanks for checking up on me. 'Preciate it. You in Leipzig?'

'Berlin. They've moved me.'

'I was supposed to become a mother last month.'

'I know. I wish I could help you.'

'I didn't manage to put away that dream as well as you did. It came back with a vengeance. The excitement. Maybe it's because you're that bit older.'

'*Ach-du-liebe-Zeit,* Suki. You're old too.'

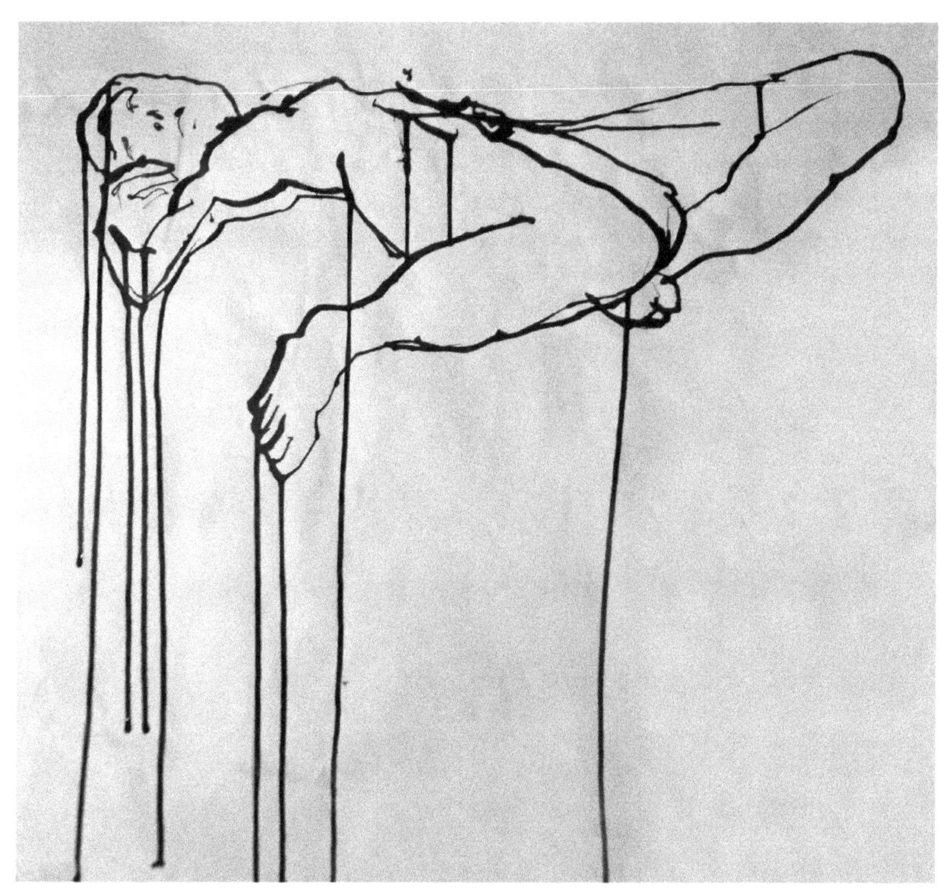

Jane Fielder

61. Option 1

And then she sends me a postcard. A sketch from the Käthe Kollwicz Museum. Our first trip. Two decades ago. The first flush of love.

Saw this and thought of you... Do you want to come and live in Berlin? I'm lonely too.

But I am a writer. German is the wrong language.

Helen Wheatley

62. Option 2

Leave that disgusting hovel and move in with me. Do my washing and ironing. Clean my toilet. Look after my household needs which will include sex on demand obviously. Do as you're told and in return you get my fabulous warm, spacious, stylish apartment to write in while I'm out working. It's win win, Suki. I want you.
Tamara
I'm lonely too.

Late at night, I notice in my spam-clogged inbox an unopened email from Bel!

Soz long silence, stuff happend, meet 4 drink b4 nex Thurs?

What day is it today? I don't know whether I'm coming or going.

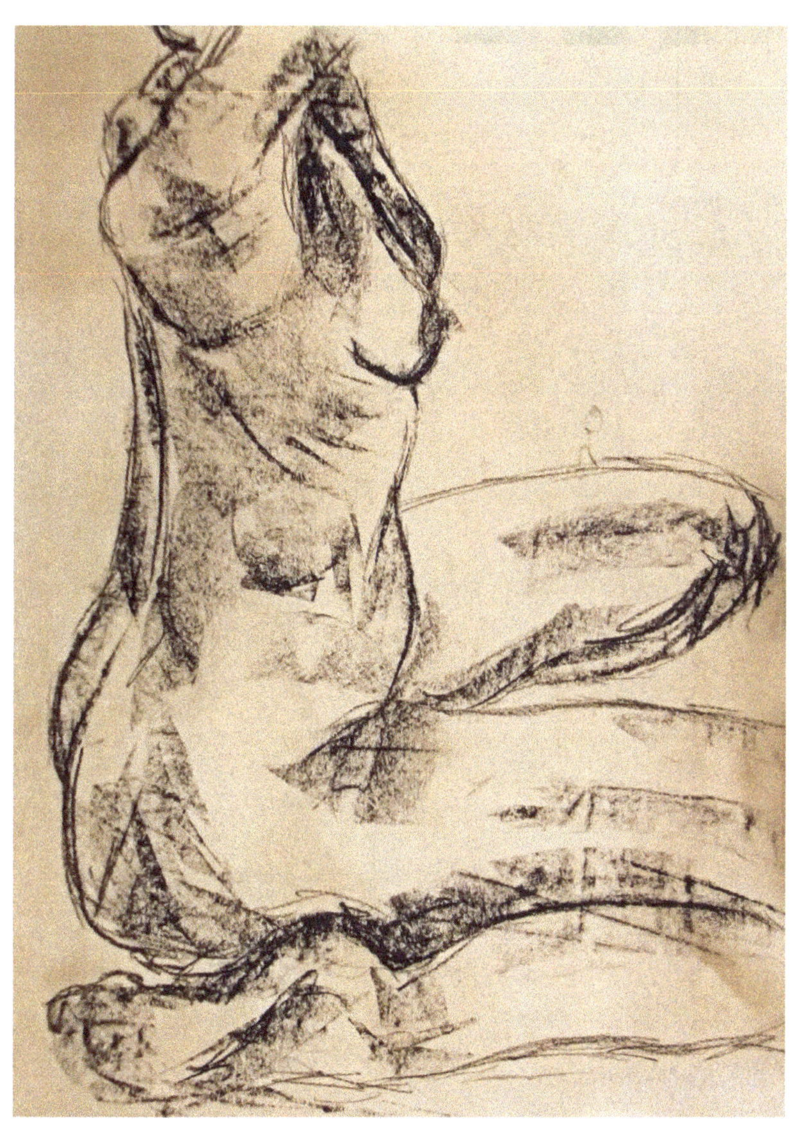

Sophie Pope

63. Option 3

A surprise text:

You about?

After everything that failed to happen, after everything that didn't get said.

For some reason, I think Bel could advise me. I think we have things in common that we've never talked about. I think she could be the person I need.

I go into my emails and answer the one I found from her last night, but get back an infuriating out-of-office reply - *I am working in Shanghai...* We are fated never to be friends.

So I formulate my answer to his text.

No, I am not about, Mister bloody bastard CJ.

But I don't send it.

Russell Lumb

64. Victoria Herz of Brown and Herz Literary Agency

She saw the Guardian review of 'Melanie Alone' and I have received her email here in Berlin. Oh to be courted by an *Überagent*!

I must decide how to reply.

Surprised to hear from you again Victoria. Yes, I am well on with my next novel...

A teensy fib.

Anyway it is a champagne moment. Champagne is cheaper here. We have found a reason for champagne most days so far.

Bill Parker

Contributing artists

John Allcock	artbyallcock.co.uk
Douglas Binder	dougjbinder.com
John Bolland	saturdaypeople.org.uk/jbolland.htm
Edith Boyer	
Carine Brosse	onceuponatimeetc.com
Lois Brothwell	loizart.co.uk
Tony Bulley	flickr.com/photos/tonybulley
Sandra Cowper	
Eliza Dear	elizadear.wordpress.com
Joan Dearnley	
Cathy Everett	
Jane Fielder	janefielder.com
Claire Gains	
Philip Hadwin	
Glenn Hall	glennhallart.wordpress.com
Fiona Halliday	fionahallidayartist.co.uk
Martin Hannavy	
Keith Hanselman	totteridgegallery.com/artist/keith-hanselman
Brenda Head	brenheadartist.co.uk
Roger Hitchen	rogerhitchen.co.uk
Sarah Hodgson	
Joanne Hogg	
Nick Holmes	
Jane Hurford	
Yvonne Hurley	
Sue Ibbotson	pinterest.com/sueibbo/my-work
Julia Jaeger	feralillustrations.com
Paul Keen	
Keith Lowe	keithlowe.co.uk
Russell Lumb	russelllumbartist.com
David Mace	
John Macfarlan	huddartsoc.webeden.co.uk/john-macfarlan
Neil Massey	
Phil Moody	philmoody.com
Colin Morgan	artistsandillustrators.co.uk/colin-john-morgan

Jill Moynan	artist-jillmoynan.webeden.co.uk
Chris Murray	chrismurray.org
Tony Noble	tonynoble-artist.com
Sheila Overton	
Patricia Oxley	
Bill Parker	artmartuk.com/yorkshire-artists/bill-parker
Helen Peyton	helenpeyton.com
Sophie Pope	
Susan Forster Ross	saturdaypeople.org.uk/sross.htm
Kate Stewart	katestewart-art.blogspot.de
David Thomas	junctionworkshop.co.uk/david_thomas
Jo Thompson	
Janey Walklin	artmartuk.com/yorkshire-artists/janey-walklin
Helen Wheatley	helenwheatley.co.uk
David Whiting	huddartsoc.webeden.co.uk/david-whiting
Emma Whiting	emmawhiting.co.uk
Tom Wood	tomwoodartist.com